Table of Contents

Tales from the Forgotten Isles........................6

Attributions

The cover image used in this work is by <u>Stefan Keller</u> from <u>Pixabay</u> and is used with permission.

Evocation

From these the coastland peoples spread in their lands,
each with his own language,
by their clans, in their nations.

Genesis 10:5

Foreword

This collection of fantasy short stories is set in another world: where magic is real; where dragons – good and bad – dominate the skies; and where other races rub shoulders with mankind in the woods, hills, and outer spaces of inhabited kingdoms.

Each short story centres upon a single main character in a unique setting. Taking their stories together, their diverse experiences and perspectives shed much colour upon the times and places in which they live.

But wait – there's more! In addition, at the end of each short story is a poem describing the main character from the narrative. This prose and poetry duet – I hope – can present a more rounded composite picture of the cultural milieux depicted in each story.

Readers interested in original creative writing are invited to connect with me via the social media links provided via my website: antipodeanwriter.wordpress.com.

Antipodean Writer
August 2020

Preface

This work is a collection of fantasy short stories and poetry.

Readers who enjoy original creative writing are invited to check out my other collections:

Prose works by Antipodean Writer

- **Orpheus Sings**
  – Short Story Collection

- **Tales of the Forgotten Isles**
  – Short Story & Poetry Collection

- **What if Jesus came Back?**
  - Eight gospel stories in modern day dress

- **When Darkness Falls**
  - Intercepted emails from an Executive Devil to a Junior Tempter

Antipodean Writer
August 2020

Tales from the Forgotten Isles

Isles

Short Story & Poetry Collection

Fregg Willows the Fisherman

Fregg lived by himself in a small reed hut nestled in a dingle close to the sea. The dingle sheltered Fregg's hut from the worst of the sea-storms that whipped the waters in the bay into a lather of foam. Most storms ceased after a day or two: then Fregg would return to the water in his small fishing-boat that he had crafted himself out of the plentiful supply of trees that grew upon his island.

Fregg had never been inland so far as to loose the sound of the sea in his ears. To him, the sea was a profound symphony: a dear companion always murmuring endearments day and night. Fregg shook his head thinking of those poor folk who contrived to live inland away from the salty brine which was his life: living inland was not for him!

Fregg sailed in all but the wildest gales: so he was well used to the ocean's moods. Like all fishermen, he knew stories of men who had taken one chance too many with the ocean: and had never returned home. Like most of his fellows, Fregg hesitated in writing off these lost ones as "dead": he thought that perhaps the Great Ocean Mother had taken them for herself, to live with her in the palatial gardens she tended in the ocean depths.

But Fregg didn't presume upon the ocean's favours: all knew the Great Mother to be notoriously capricious. Drowned bodies – sometimes washed up upon the sands after a fierce gale – were likely "lost ones" expelled from her domain: those who had displeased the Great Ocean Mother. Though such gruesome finds were infrequent, they did serve to make the fisher-folk careful in all their ocean-going business.

Thus Fregg too was a careful fisherman. Until one evening when he saw the were-lights.

Fregg was fishing one day under overcast skies: his weather-sense telling him that that a gale was approaching. Fregg had been fishing late, and had just secured his gear before trimming the sails to make for home. His boat had begun moving forwards when he saw them: lights of a myriad of colours, dancing upon the surface of the sea - like sparkling jewels in motion.

The were-lights were on his way, so Fregg needed to alter course only slightly for a closer look. The were-lights danced and jumped about like living things: becoming more entrancing the closer he came. Fregg was enchanted by their colourful motions: he had never seen such beauty before.

It was getting darker – but Fregg pursued the lights as they leapt and bobbed onwards across the sea. One part of Fregg's mind noted that by following the were-lights he was changing course - his boat was now leaving the isle behind and heading into the open sea. But Fregg pushed all such thoughts away, for the were-lights were close now: what colours! What shapes!

The were-lights danced and weaved, and allowed the fisherman to sail into their midst. Fregg took no notice of the wind beginning to howl in the teeth of the arriving storm. The were-lights continued to circle in delightful patterns, and Fregg sailed on and on into the night...

The gale lasted four days: so violent that no fisherman caught at sea could possibly have survived. Fregg Willow's neighbours noted that Fregg hadn't returned before the gale struck: but there was nothing they could do. The Great Ocean Mother had taken another lost-one to her bosom. Such things happened.

But several days later, two fisher-men brought back an oar they had found adrift on the seas about the isle. Most of the villagers reckoned the oar was made by Fregg – it showed the signs of his craft – but for a different reason the oar quickly became the centre of attention for everyone in that village and all the other villages nearby. For embedded in the blade of that plain, wooden oar was a small circled-crown made of pure gold.

The identity of the oar's owner generated a welcome controversy that raged for months: most couldn't believe the oar was really Fregg's, for all who knew him knew he was as poor as themselves. But a stolid minority persisted in pointing out that the oar was made by Fregg himself – as anybody could see who knew Fregg's handicraft. But none could explain the embedded gold-crown. Perhaps it was a gift from the Great Ocean Mother?

While the arguments raged back and forth; one cantankerous, old woman called them all a pack of know-nothing fools: holding forth stridently that the gold-crown was the undoubted sign of the sea-faeries – therefore it was they, and nobody else, who taken Fregg away with them, and the oar had been returned to signify Fregg was living among them. The old woman's tone was fierce and her tongue sharp, and no-one argued against her when she was present. But when she had left everyone recalled among themselves that she was widowed and had lived many years alone, and was fey in consequence: so no-one believed her.

The oar was finally laid to rest inside a grassy mound outside Fregg's tiny fishing-village; and is spoken of to this day as the resting-place of Fregg's Oar. The mound is covered with lush, green grass in all seasons: and is climbed all over by the younger village children during their outdoor games.

Fregg was never seen again by the fisher-folk. But many still think him to be alive and well cared for, wherever he might be.

A Boating Song

Ah-yee! Feel the waves -

Current running, waters lave.

Ah-yee! Sun and moon -

Follow fishes, catch some soon.

Wind in sail, rudder steer -

Daylight, moonlight, through the year.

Fill the nets and pull the line.

Boating, sailing: wet or fine.

Ah-yee! Turn for home.

Trim the sails, cut the foam!

Ah-yee! Sailing-boat -

Water-horse so fine afloat.

Phillignea the Shrine Priestess

Phillignea lived alone at the small shrine: dividing her efforts between keeping the grounds tidy and her duties as the shrine's priestess. She often had visitors, for Phillignea's simple magic could cure common ailments and diseases, and bless herds with fertility and increase. She never left the shrine: she had been abandoned there as a baby orphan and raised by her predecessor, the old priestess before her. She had called the old priestess "mother", and the shrine had always been her home. She had buried the old priestess many years ago and become priestess in her place. She was still hale and strong, her chestnut hair flowing in waves over her shoulders whenever she left it unbound, on days like today.

Phillignea knew everything that went on in the island: certainly her visitors kept her supplied with the local gossip. But the priestess had other ways to find things out: the women guessed she used birds as her eyes and ears – and this might have been true, for Phillignea often walked about the shrine gardens with wild birds perched upon an arm or shoulder, talking to them quietly. And anyway – what else could they think? For Phillignea never told anyone about The Chair of Seeing.

The Chair was kept in a small chamber at the top of the shrine's fane which the old priestess had always kept locked; until just before the end when she willingly surrendered her duties into Phillignea's charge. Only then was Phillignea allowed into the chamber: which was small and walled with stone, and held little besides the large stone chair placed at its centre: The Chair of Seeing. By sitting on this chair Phillignea was shown how she could see any part of the island by just focusing her concentration. Her first Seeing had quickly left her drained and exhausted: but the old priestess had assured her that endurance came with practice – and now Phillignea could undertake Seeing for extended periods.

So, when the chores were done, and she had no visitors – Phillignea would often retire to the small chamber and go Seeing. She eventually discovered a few places that The Chair could not take her – presumably they were protected by some magic stronger than her own. But there was little else that happened anywhere upon the island that remained hidden from her questing eyes for long.

One evening in late autumn, Phillignea noted a strange trading-ship harboured in her island's single port. The ship's colours and markings were strange – but her attention was soon drawn to a passenger disembarking, and beginning to amble towards the inn set aside for visitors to the island. Focusing her attention to approach the man more closely, it was only a few moments before she cried out in surprise, and broke the Seeing: finding herself seated upon The Chair in the small stone chamber, her body trembling. For the man had turned about and looked straight towards her – and had seen her. Phillignea was stunned: this had never happened before. Until today, she always had been invisible and undetectable during a Seeing. Until today.

When Phillignea left the chamber she went to bed, for it was late: but not to sleep. She remained troubled by the strange visitor to the island, who could see her while she was Seeing. Who was he?

The next day she noted that the strange trading-ship was still in the harbour. The man was not at the inn – so she quickly checked each street of the little town, before extending her search more widely. Eventually she found him, walking along a well-used track, leaving the port behind and leading a carrier-beast which carried a woman nursing a baby. They were following the path that led to the foothills below her own mountain.

She observed from a discreet distance for some time, before withdrawing reluctantly and breaking the Seeing: she had chores to do. But all morning her mind wandered. She watched the shadows cast by the shrine walls mark the hours. Perhaps he would arrive later in the day?

That afternoon, she sat once more on The Chair to observe the party arrive at where the path plateaued, just a mile or two away from the entrance to her shrine. The man stopped to rest the beast and speak to the woman. Then, straightening, he turned slowly about until he faced the vantage point Phillignea had chosen: and raised an arm in greeting. Phillignea gasped and broke the Seeing, her heart pounding. She left the chamber hurriedly: feeling confused and excited. He had seen her again. Who was he?

When the party arrived Phillignea didn't forget her role as priestess: and made the ritual greetings at the shrine's entrance flawlessly, despite her burning curiosity. She noted the lines of sadness about the man's eyes, that the woman was much younger than he, and that the baby was asleep. The man returned her greeting kindly, the woman said nothing at all – staring wide-eyed about her all the while.

Inside the shrine, the man helped the woman dismount and settled her comfortably in a garden seat. After securing the carrier-beast, he looked about and saw Phillignea waiting for him. He approached with a quiet smile, saying "Good health to you Phillignea." Phillignea was surprised that he knew her name – she had not told them, but had introduced herself only as the shrine's priestess; as custom required.

The man was no longer young, but his glance was keen and he noted her reaction. "Have they told you nothing at all, Phillignea?" he asked, gently. "Is it possible that you do not know why we – I and the wet-nurse – are here?" When the priestess shook her head, speechless, the man sighed and took her arm and guided them to where they might sit out of earshot but remain in sight of the wet-nurse, who was now suckling the babe.

"I had hoped..." he started to say, and then looking into her face, he stopped. "With your permission, priestess," he began again, more soberly.

"Phillignea – please..." smiled Phillignea somewhat timidly. The man returned the smile, a little sadly.

"Phillignea. Let me start from the beginning." And as the man began to speak, Phillignea forgot about her surroundings, and the island, and was carried away upon the gentle stream of words that flowed on and on – and told her so many things that she had never known nor even suspected...

The man took the wet-nurse and left three days later, just as soon as one of the island-women could be found to suckle the baby in her stead. They returned to the trading-ship, which weighed anchor and sailed on the next tide. Phillignea was upon The Chair Seeing them depart: the tears coursing down her cheeks, until eventually the sails merged with the horizon.

After the babe was weaned, Phillignea cared for it herself. In the years that followed, many noted that the priestess was often silent and thoughtful. The gossips remarked much upon the mysterious origins of the orphan child she was raising: and as the priestess never confided in anyone, they speculated freely. Although never in Phillignea's company.

And the orphan girl continued to grow under Phillignea's care, and lived with her in the mountain shrine.

Song of Seeing

The priestess, ringed by her walls of stone

Sits down alone, in a quiet zone.

Her Seeing views all deeds afar

From atop the mountain shrine.

Do the patterned leaves speak to the air?

The trees are there. Their soughings fair.

She Seeing comes to walk afar

Then return to the mountain shrine.

Through the air she comes and goes unseen

Through walls between, ethereal queen.

She Seeing within while still afar

Seated in the mountain shrine.

And Seeing she has come to know

Where people go, the face they show.

By Seeing all yet from afar

From her seat in the mountain shrine.

Tusselldorf the Bandit

Tusselldorf munched steadily. He had worked up an appetite during his long overnight march: now he could enjoy a long rest out of the sun. He had put several leagues between himself and any possible pursuit – but he did not think there would be any. Why would soldiers bother to follow a lone brigand over steep goat-tracks, trying to track him down to some remote mountain-retreat? Tusseldorf's lips curled disdainfully at the thought, as he washed down his repast with a skin of wine.

Of course, from time to time a bounty-hunter came along: these were more persistent than mere soldiers. But bounty-hunters had had no luck with him. Tusselldorf chuckled at the memories: no human could close with a dwarf in mountain-country.

Like all dwarves, Tusselldorf was short, stocky, and very strong. He had taken refuge in the mountain ranges years ago: ever since being cast out by his clan for his part in a revenge-kinslaying. After his expulsion, he had trekked east and turned to a life of brigandage. His life was hard: but dwarf's bones are like iron, and their flesh endures extremes far better than those of mens – so he got by well enough. Unlike the human bandits round about, Tusselldorf has no personal quarrel with anyone and was not malicious: he fought only to defend himself, which was not often. Usually he simply took what he wanted – those he robbed being too terrified to resist - and vanished.

Tusseldorf sighed. He was getting bored with banditry. Perhaps he should return west and join another clan: as his own would no longer accept him. His dwarven hands longed once more to forge metals and jewels into beautiful shapes, such as: swords, furniture, lampstands... He was a good craftsman still: he knew it in his bones.

The dwarf shrugged off his pack and sat down, making himself comfortable. He would sleep soon. His fingers fished about in his multitudinous pockets to pull out a beautiful jewelled casket. The precious stones flashed and sparkled in the sunlight, awaking a deep pleasure in Tusselldorf. Dwarves always appreciated fine workmanship.

The casket had been taken earlier from a boy dressed in outlandish clothes, driving a horse and laden cart along one of the roads near the forest Tusselldorf frequented. The boy was alone and Tusselldorf halted him as a matter of course. The boy protested that he was a wizard's apprentice – but had not resisted when the dwarf curtly ordered him to dismount and stand by the road. The boy looked downcast when Tusselldorf recovered the casket from beneath the driver's seat: the boy mumbled that the casket was magic, and that he would regret taking it. Tusselldorf laughed hugely at the boy's words and jumped down from the cart. The booming voice of the dwarf startled the cart-horse, who jerked into a gallop down the road, with the boy running along behind, shouting at the horse to stop. With a parting grin, the dwarf vanished from sight: trekking steadily up into the mountains.

Now at rest, Tusselldorf hesitated before opening the casket. Dwarves are by nature suspicious of wizards: commonly holding them to be meddlers in things but poorly understood. But the casket's gold and jewels called to him in the sunshine. Shrugging aside his doubts, Tusselldorf's strong hands gently opened the lid; and he looked inside...

---oOo---

The wizard located Tusselldorf a few days later. The dwarf was still seated in the glade, unmoving as a marble statue. The dwarf's eyes were open but unblinking, as he gazed into the depths of the enchanted casket. The apprentice had, of course, by this time told his master what had befallen him on the road: so the wizard had set out to reclaim what belonged to him. By his own magic arts he had discovered the glade where the dwarf had been frozen into immobility.

The wizard looked down at the dwarf awhile, with an unreadable expression upon his face. Sighing deeply, he raised his staff and brought its tip down gently upon the crown of Tusselldorf's head. The dwarf's eyes blinked, then closed as his body tumbled gently onto its side. The slack hands released the casket - which would have fallen onto the ground except the wizard quickly gathered it up: closing it and securing it within the folds of his robe.

The dwarf began to snore. The wizard smiled, and departed.

---oOo---

Tusselldorf awoke much later: feeling the chill air presaging sunrise. He scratched his head absent-mindedly, and stood up. His belly grumbled with unexpected urgency – as though it had remained empty for a week.

Shaking his head, Tusselldorf tried to recall what had happened. An image formed in his mind of a casket – an enchanted casket – full of demon-wizardry...

Tusselldorf was strong – even in his present weakened state: but as the memories of what he had seen inside the casket flooded his mind, he staggered and remained leaning weakly against a tree-trunk so that he didn't fall over. He began shuddering uncontrollably.

It took some time for the feelings to pass. When they did, Tusselldorf hefted his pack and – with a resolute set to his shoulders - strode out of the glade. He ate while he walked westwards – away from the mountains that bordered the lands of men.

Tusselldorf was never seen again in those parts. It cannot be said that he was greatly missed.

A Smithing Song

Swing the hammer, shape the blade -

Leaping flames about it played.

Heat it, beat it, beat it down.

Shape it. Beauty efforts crown.

Silver, gold and precious stones -

Jewellery and bracelets hone.

Spear-points, shields, knives to hue,

Arrow-heads and sword-blades true.

Mine it, dig it underground -

Pickaxe, shovel, veins abound.

Copper, tin and iron bring

Heat the forge! Let hammers ring!

The Mergrill Children

The brother moaned quietly as he lay on his bed. It was night, and the boy lay in his room inside a small cottage. The village was some miles away, and hidden from sight. The moon was out and shining brightly – although the boy could not see it. His eyes remained closed, and he moaned as he wandered through some dream-world of his own: as he did most nights.

His sister sat by his bedside and held his hand. He was all she had, for their parents had died two years ago; and they knew of no other kindred: except vaguely that some lived but far away – they knew not exactly where. The sister knew her brother was unaware of her presence, but she liked to be nearby when his dreams came upon. As they so often did, now.

She sat, looking out his window towards the wood, watching the moon travel gracefully though the night sky. The boy moaned again, and she squeezed his hand a little, reassuringly.

Daytime was easier. During the day, her brother would wake and eat some broth. His skin was grey and he needed her arm to walk any distance: but he willingly did whatever he could. She feared for him now, and he too was afraid: afraid that soon he would sicken and sink down into dream-lands and not have strength enough to return to the lands of the living.

The girl was practical: she kept the house and weeded the garden, and tended their cow – whom they called Jersey. Jersey always greeted her by turning her large head: the girl imagined the cow's deep, liquid eyes were wise, and understanding.

During the day her brother soon tired, and would lie down again. He suffered no pain, but his lethargy and lack of appetite disabled him from enjoying the normal life boys of his age should lead. When he lay down, he would fight against falling asleep; to avoid tumbling again into the dream-world. Sometimes he would speak about it: once he found himself in a labyrinth of stone, seeking for the exit that would fit a diamond key he clutched tightly in his hand. Another time he walked alone through a city of endless streets – walking around and around, trying to find the gate to let himself outside to freedom...

"I'm nearly there!" her brother had whispered to her perhaps a week ago just after he awoke from another troubled night. She had smiled a little, to encourage him to talk some more. "I nearly found the way out! If only I had someone to guide me through the maze..." he continued, his voice a strange mixture of dreamy triumph and despair. She heard him in silence, listening to him describe the terrible dream-world that seemed to be consuming his strength, leaving him a shadow. She tried to be strong for his sake, but she shuddered whenever she thought about his horrid dream-world, and wished someone would appear to lead him back again to health, and the daylight.

The village had forgotten the existence of the two children: but the old farmer and his wife who lived nearby had not. The old couple had known the children's parents and befriended them, despite the fact they were from foreign parts. When first the mother, then the father had caught the marsh-fever sweeping through the country-side; the farmer's wife had nursed them as they lay dying. The old farmer had promised the parents they would care for their children: and when the parents had been laid in shallow graves near the wood, he invited the children to come and live with them. However, the children wanted to remain in their parents' cottage: so the farmer's wife became an almost daily visitor. She would talk with the sister, assist with chores; and every week the old farmer too would come and help out. And so the old couple and the young siblings took from each other what comfort they could: and genuine affection grew up between them.

It was late spring and the farmer's wife was leaving the village for home, when a stranger approached her to bid her good morning: she having been pointed out to him by one of the shopkeepers. The stranger came up and introduced himself in a soft-spoken manner; and asked where the Mergrills lived. "Nass and Drew are dead." answered the farmer's wife, shaking her head. The stranger's face became sad and downcast. When she told him that their children still lived, he brightened and asked for directions. The woman replied that she would lead him there herself, as she was going to stop by on her way home. She didn't show her surprise in anyone asking after the children: she had taken a liking to the stranger, and believed he meant no harm.

Arriving at the cottage, the man stepped in after the farmer's wife, and the sister rose and stared past the woman straight at the stranger. The old wife turned towards the visitor to introduce him, but gave a small cry and fell silent: for as a stray sunbeam fell upon the stranger through the cottage window he seemed for a moment to be completely different from the plain-clothed traveller she had met. For one moment he appeared taller, clothed in armour with a sword belted at his side, holding a gold helmet in one hand... She blinked, and the illusion was gone: only an ordinary-looking man dressed in plain homespun stood there speaking to the sister in soft, well-mannered tones.

The old woman made herself busy and looked in at the brother lying on his bed. The man continued speaking earnestly with the sister in the main living area. The farmer's wife thought she heard a sprinkle of words in a foreign tongue that she didn't understand: but their voices were kept low, so she wasn't certain. After a time, the sister took the woman outside to help her with weeding the garden; leaving the man alone inside the cottage sitting beside the brother's bedside. Even outside the women could hear the man talking quietly to the boy on the bed, and sometimes it seemed as if the boy answered him. Something unusual was happening: the old woman could sense it.

When the farmer's wife asked the sister about it, the latter replied absently, "The man is showing my brother how to escape the dream-world and return to the daylight." and refused to say any more. The old woman let her be, and became thoughtful.

It was getting dark, and the sister had returned inside. When the old woman finally stopped and thought of gathering her things together, she considered stopping for the night – her husband was away for a few days, and it was too late for her to get home. She started towards the cottage door when a tremendous crack like thunder, followed by a dazzling flash of light came from the boy's window. The old woman collapsed to her knees, terrified. Soon she felt arms gently helping her to her feet, leading her inside and speaking soothingly to dispel her disquiet. She wasn't aware who helped her – she was in shock: so she remained still and silent, and was left in peace awhile.

She soon recovered however, and looking around, saw that the house was empty and dark. Not that that worried her - for she knew the inside of their cottage as well as her own. But she began wondering where the children were. The children!

Outside a bonfire was blazing: so the old woman came to the door and saw the sister and her brother standing near the fire with the stranger nearby. She gasped in surprise: for all three were now dressed in outlandish garb, and the boy stood tall and strong – looking healthier than she had ever seen him. Hearing her, the children flew to her side and hugged her, and brought her close to the stranger who smiled at her kindly.

The sister pressed something soft into her hand, and whispered farewell. The old woman couldn't understand what was happening: she hung onto the boy and kept murmuring "Why – you're well again! So strong!" And the boy grinned and laughed, while his sister explained that the stranger had freed him from his bewitching dreams; and had come to take them both across the sea, back to their own kindred.

Uncomprehending, the old woman accepted their good-bye hugs and words; and looked on as all three walked off into the night across the barley field. Everything was dark except a couple of small flames that seemed to dance above the ground like fairy-lights. There was silence for awhile, before the sounds of a huge beast was heard – invisible in the darkness – and the shouted farewells from the girl and the boy. Finally, with a great noise, a large shape launched itself skywards, circling the house once, twice, three times on immense wings: and when the dragon passed across the moon's face the old woman thought she saw huddled upon its neck small human shapes waving down at her. Then they were gone.

The old woman collapsed by the warm fire, overcome with conflicting emotions. Slowly she became aware of the thing she still held in her hand. The farmer's wife looked at it curiously by the firelight: it was a small case made of cloth dyed a rich blue, which opened to reveal some jewelled bracelets and a necklace so valuable they could buy up the entire village. The woman stared at the stones twinkling in the firelight, before looking up and into the night sky. She was silent for a long time.

The Mergrill children had gone: they would never return to the cottage. They were going home.

Dragon Flight

Our scaly beast on airy wings pursues the wind

Its slitted eyes take yellow-glances at the moon

Its scales gleam and sparkle in the soft moonbeams

We dragon ride.

      To see a home we've never seen

Returning to our people from across the sea

Led on by hope. A dragon-song we sing tonight

Beneath the moon and stars we sing aloud for joy.

The dragon skims the waves, delighted by the sea

And soars aloft to catch the warming streams of air

To sail along. We catch our breath in dragon-flight.

And soon – so soon – the spires of our people's town

Will come to view. The home we lost will soon be found

And recompense for years of tears at last be made.

The dragon flies. We crouch into his scaly hide.

He swoops. And soars. We ride the dragon wind tonight.

Egridelas' Scouting

The elves had their hands full for a time, hunting down the marauders who had marched confidently into their forests some few days before. The marauders were mainly heavily-armed men from Maghreb – led by a few trolls and orcs. The trolls were the hardest to kill: always needing to be cut down, no matter how many arrows pierced their stinking hides. No quarter was asked – or given.

When the last of the invaders had fallen, their bodies were heaped up and burned. While the smoke rose, light-footed scouts crossed and re-crossed the miles all the way to the forest edge to ensure that none had escaped. During this activity they joyfully recovered one of their own, Egridelas, lying concealed: having lost much blood from an orc-arrow to his upper arm. Egridelas had been posted on lookout at the edge of their forest: his was the first horn to raise the alarm. He had not returned to the host before the main battle, and grave fears had been held for his safety.

Egridelas was fevered, for the orc-arrow had been poisoned. His companions hurried him back to the main body before contriving for him a stretcher: then carried him deep into the forests where the elvan strongholds are.

As it turned out, Egridelas lived: although he was unconscious by the time the healers neutralised the poison. When he awoke it was early morning, and an healer sat nearby – watching him. Smiling gently, the healer spoke softly and answered his questions: giving him a strong herbal drink and changing his dressings.

When alone, Egridelas drew strength from his surroundings inside the Halls of Healing. He watched the sunshine dance along the walls, and listened to the whispers of the healers, and the elf-maidens who worked alongside them.

That afternoon he had a visitor – Frithaleed, a friend who had been at the battle. Frithaleed sat by his bed and related everything while Egridelas listened. "Not one escaped us!" related Frithaleed proudly. "Your warning gave us time to meet them before they even crossed the river!"

Egridelas grinned appreciatively, and remembered to keep his arm still: for it hurt to move it. "I wish I had been there with the main host," he said. "I shot down two of them before..." and he nodded towards his wounded arm. His arm muscles throbbed dully – it was a wound that would take time to heal.

"You will live to fight another day," laughed Frithaleed. Then they spoke upon lighter matters until one of the elf-maidens came to shoo the visitor away. When Frithaleed had left, she returned to bring Egridelas something to eat and drink, flashing him a radiant smile as she left.

Egridelas refreshed himself, before dozing and beginning to dream. In his dreams he found himself swimming and laughing with friends in the great waterfalls outside Lithlorien: clambering among the slippery rocks and exploring the shallow caves that pitted the mountain stones, many hidden behind cascading water.

He was asleep when the elf-maid returned to stand by his bed and gaze down at him with a tender expression on her beautiful features. Quickly she bent down and kissed his forehead lightly, before clearing away his bedside table and leaving him alone once more.

Egridelas remained still. Then he murmured softly in his sleep, his lips twitching into a faint smile.

Song of the Arrow

Feathered shaft and steel-tip,

Fly where you're sped!

Down the kill to feast whereby,

Cleave the skies!

Kill the meat, for my hearth

Winging the wind.

Straight your shaft, arrow mine,

Fly! Strike true!

Pierce the shield, shatter bone,

Bring foes down!

Through helm, piercing armour,

Slay foes dead.

The Quest of Brenn Bragdolhaed

The skull loomed out of the darkness, grinning as it began to make a low, evil, chuckling sound. Angrily, Brenn drew his sword and slashed – but his blade met with no resistance, and whistled through empty air. The skull vanished when the sword touched it, but the low, chuckling continued. Brenn was not afraid of phantoms: they could not touch him or cause him hurt. He scorned their attempts to frighten him, but he was tired. His body complained of growing, physical exhaustion.

Brenn was lost underground in the Kaarg Labyrinth. He could not find a way out. His food was gone and nearly all his water. Would there be water underground? Perhaps. But first he would need to find it. And soon his last torch would go out, leaving him alone in the darkness. With phantoms for company...

Brenn had been lost for days – he didn't know how many, for here time had no meaning. His companions might still be waiting for him at the labyrinth's entrance: but he had expressly forbidden them – under oath - to attempt a rescue. Kaarg had already swallowed too many good men.

When Brenn first realised that he was lost, he had yelled and cried out: hoping to hear his friends' answer so that he could guide himself back to the surface. But the echoes underground had distorted his cries into a thousand mockeries, bouncing back at him from every direction. Besides – he admitted to himself with a grimace – it was unlikely that his friends could actually hear him at all.

Brenn tried to comfort himself with the thought that death lay across all paths these days: especially since the orc-raids had begun. They fought back – arming even their boys as warriors and their women as shield-maidens. They had fought well: but their enemies were many while they were few. It was only a matter of time before they were overwhelmed.

But Brenn knew – as all did – the legends about Kaarg. In the Kaarg Labyrinths the Old Kings had hidden their powerful magic – some said in scrolls, others in enchanted rings or swords. The power of the Old Kings had been strong enough to protect their people even from dragons. And Brenn's people desperately needed that sort of protection: needed it to survive the orc-raids that became more brazen with every passing year.

Brenn knew that the Old Kings were as just and as good as they were powerful: they had set up these phantoms to scare away common thieves. But for Brenn, the phantoms confirmed that the power of the Old Kings he sought still remained hidden in the Kaarg Labyrinth. Somewhere. If only he could find it...

Brenn's torch went out at last. So Brenn sat down in the darkness to drink his last few mouthfuls of water. There was no other sound apart from his own breathing. He was alone. Lost underground. In darkness.

Undaunted, Brenn moved about on the cold, rocky floor to make himself comfortable and rest. His body was tired out from his frantic exertions to find the exit before his torch failed. But now, he had all the time in the world. There was no more need for haste.

Tomorrow, when he woke, he would move by touch, straining to hear the least sound that might give him some clue as to the right direction to take. With this thought in mind, Brenn wrapped himself up in a thick cloak, and went to sleep.

---oOo---

"How much longer should we wait?" asked Hurg. Rinn looked glum, and said nothing. Hurg threw some more wood upon the fire, before continuing. "Brenn told us to wait no more than four days. We've been here seven."

Rinn spat into the flames and spoke gruffly. "Maybe time to go in after him."

Hurg looked up angrily. "Not against my oath!" Rinn glared back challengingly for a moment: but then his shoulders slumped in defeat and he looked away.

"Brenn's not coming out." said Hurg, quietly. "We've got to go back. Kill us some more orcs." As Rinn didn't reply, Hurg turned around and composed himself for sleep. Rinn remained seated, staring into the flames until dawn: straining his ears for a sound – any sound – from the labyrinth entrance that would signal that Brenn was still alive...

---oOo---

The next morning Hurg and Rinn started on their return journey. They travelled carefully to avoid the attentions of marauders.

The Kaarg labyrinth behind them maintained its brooding silence; keeping its secrets to itself - wrapped in darkness.

A Sword Song

Slash the blade and make it sing -

Whirl the blade and flash the steel.

Parry, thrust, then cut and sting -

Death-strokes deal.

Sing a sword-song, music make -

Hack the foeman, hew him down.

Slake your thirst in orcish blood -

Bloodthirst drown.

Flash the steel, whirl the blade,

Fighting, force the bandits back.

Hew their limbs and lend all aid

Press attack.

Blooded, whetted, cease to thrust -

Aftermath of waiting, keening.

Foes are dead, now rest you must -

Death has meaning.

Life has meaning.

The Boy by the Sea

Osprey Jeln was a small boy, who lived alone with an aunt in a village close to the sea. Most of his time was spent amongst the ancient Barrow Downs outside the village. Osprey's aunt fed and clothed him – but otherwise treated him as a nuisance and told him to keep out of her way. Which suited Osprey well enough; for he had no affection for his aunt, nor she for him.

Osprey's father had crewed for a merchant trader two years ago and had never returned: he might be dead – drowned maybe - or be captured to be sold as a slave in some foreign port. His mother had died in childbirth six months after his father had gone to sea, leaving Osprey alone.

All the other village boys were bigger than Osprey. He was constantly being picked upon: the village men either ignored what was happening or slyly encouraged their boys in their efforts. Osprey avoided the village as a rule, retreating to the barrows – for the villagers were affrighted of the old burial grounds, and even during the day gave the barrows a wide berth.

As a result the barrows became Osprey's place of refuge. He climbed atop them and spent hours gazing longingly out to sea. He play between them, building stone forts and conducting miniature battles. He didn't know much about the barrows: he had overhead some stories that they were connected with the legendary Sea Kings: half-pirates, half-warlords, who had ruled by the sea with a strong arm for over a century until their line failed, and their lands fell into other hands.

When one day Osprey noticed a small opening in the front of one of the larger barrows that he hadn't seen before, he kept the knowledge to himself. There was no point in telling his aunt – or anyone else in the village for that matter. But a plan suggested itself to Osprey – and he hugged himself in excitement. Even his aunt's usual scolding that evening failed to quench his mood as he took himself to bed.

The following day he returned, bringing a flint and a torch. Using makeshift tools he widened the opening until it was big enough for his lithe body to squeeze through. Lighting a torch, Osprey wiggled through and stepped into the barrow: his body tingling with excitement for what he might find.

The barrow inside was dark and cold: his torchlight played upon the smooth walls and the rough flagstones, showing him stone carvings still with traces of faint colouring. The barrow inside was larger than his aunt's cottage, and divided mid-way by a stone partition. Gazing his fill at the walls of the front half of the chamber – whose carvings he couldn't at all understand, and which was otherwise empty - Osprey went forward slowly to the partition. An increasing sensation of dread made every hair on his neck stand upright as he reached it. Osprey forced himself to peer slowly around the partition into the second chamber.

The next thing that happened was that Osprey screamed and sprang backwards, tumbling over and dropping his torch. Osprey recovered himself quickly, grabbing the torch before it went out, and then stood upright holding the torch in front of him to ward off the foe. Breathing hard, with the blood pounding through his temples; Osprey listened for the slightest sound of movement from the dead chamber. After an interminable period of waiting – and hearing nothing except his own laboured breathing - Osprey plucked up his courage enough to tip-toe forwards and hazard another look.

It soon became clear that what Osprey had at first supposed to be eyes staring back at him were in fact dull reflections from something made of metal. Gaining confidence, he stepped forward: this chamber differed from the first, in that it contained two large platforms of raised stone. Each platform supported a corpse – presumably of one of the Sea-Kings: their skeletal remains clothed in ancient-looking mail, badly worn by time. Their arms were crossed across sunken chests, and one had a sheathed sword by his side.

Taking his time to examine everything carefully, Osprey discovered most of the metal objects were fragile and now useless. But there was one exception: a cracked leather sheath yielded a hunting-knife made from some strange metal Osprey had never seen: it was still clear of rust and quite sharp, and along its blade were carved intricate patterns that Osprey couldn't make out by torch-light. Shivering with excitement, Osprey retreated slowly to the dividing wall, carrying his new knife. Before going further, on impulse the boy turned around and bowed to each of his dead benefactors – mumbling his gratitude: no-one these days ever gave him presents. Osprey's heart suddenly lightened: he knew the dead Sea-Kings had understood. On leaving the barrow he was in high good humour.

Slithering back into the sunlight, he didn't see the man waiting for him until he literally ran into him. The man grabbed and held him, but Osprey twisted like an eel and – greatly daring – drew his new knife back ready to strike. He was tired of being beaten and bullied by the others in the village – and now they dared to follow him here! Let their blood flow for a change!

The man dropped his grip but otherwise didn't move, and Osprey stumbled backwards, off-balance. The boy then froze as the man said softly, "Jarlon."

Jarlon was Osprey's real name – but nobody used it: few even remembered it. Osprey looked wildly at the man: a glance showed him a man dressed simply, but in clothes never worn by the villagers. He was from foreign parts, his face was earnest but kind; and he reminded Osprey of someone...

"Father!"

They held each other for a long time. Osprey couldn't help himself: he cried out his loneliness, and fear, and relief. His father never spoke a word, but just held him tightly.

When they eventually they sat down at the entrance to the barrow – the father apparently taking as little notice of village prejudice as Osprey himself did - they talked for a long time. Much of what Osprey felt about the village the father had already guessed: Osprey's aunt had never liked her sister's husband, and her mislike had transferred from the father to his son. Osprey for his part hung upon every word his father spoke: how his merchant-ship had been attacked and the crew sold as slaves at Osk. How he had later escaped, stolen a ship and piloted her singled-handed back over the sea. He had called briefly at Osprey's aunt's cottage, and then come to the barrows to look for him.

It was late afternoon as they sat munching on some food that father had brought in a satchel. "Is there anything you want to get before we go?" said his father. Osprey tightened his grasp upon his new knife – his only treasure, a farewell gift from the Sea Kings - and shook his head.

His father stood and helped Osprey to his feet. His arm stayed around the boy's shoulders as they walked back through the village. Osprey feared nobody as the pair walked down the length of the main street, and they were not molested. The other villagers ignored them: not even a man escaped from slavery could move their sympathy.

As his father led Osprey down to the harbour where a trim little boat awaited them, Osprey's heart thrilled: he had never sailed before, though he had often dreamed of doing so. And now he was finally going to learn – and his own father would teach him!

"I came back to get you as soon as I could," his father said, a little ruefully as they set off. Osprey was already getting comfortable aboard – he laughed at his father's words in pure delight.

When they set sail, some of the villagers stood in the street and stared after them in silence. But neither Osprey nor his father ever looked back.

Sail Ho!

Sail-ho! Sail-ho!

Cross the waves with sunlight bright'ning

Chase the clouds with jaggéd lightning.

Sail-ho! Sail-ho!

Leave the beach and quay behind us

Trip the waves so none may find us.

Sail-ho! Sail-ho!

Seas are blue and wind is slack'ning

Skies are grey and waves are flat'ning.

Sail-ho! Sail-ho!

Gulls and whales, dolphins near us

None may follow, fear will leave us.

Sail-ho! Sail-ho!

Sail-ho!

Old Fire-eye

Old Fire-eye awoke early one morning. He scratched his empty belly and shifted position uneasily on the floor of his cave. He was hungry.

Breathing deeply, he slowly expelled the air from his nostrils. Cat-like eyes flicked around the cavern to rest lightly upon every gem he possessed in turn. Only after having satisfied himself that all was in place, Old Fire-Eye huffed happily towards the cave's entrance to stand for a moment in the cool morning air.

He must eat: he hadn't eaten for days. He would need to fly somea distance first – for nearby were only a few stringy mountain-goats: too bony to be worth chasing.

Bringing his entire bulk into the sunlight, he stretched luxuriously before leaping into the air and letting his wings take him aloft. For Old Fire-eye, of course, was a dragon.

Not that Fire-Eye was old for a dragon – as a matter of fact, in dragon-years he was still a youngster. Nor was his real name "Fire-eye" - only the hapless islanders he preyed upon called him that. His real name – his dragon-name – was known to none but himself. The islanders just didn't know any better: so, to them, he was referred to as Old Fire-Eye. Not that the dragon cared.

The dragon hummed with pleasure. Soon all the humans would be gone: leaving behind their delicious herds of cattle and sheep as they fled his island. Men could be so troublesome. They would hurt him if they could: many had tried (and failed), but they might get lucky. Worse, they could again try to steal his treasure: in fact, it was in retribution for the latest attempt that Old Fire-Eye had begun to systematically destroy each and every human habitation upon the island.

The sooner the island was his – and his alone – the better. Besides, if food became scarce he could always fly further afield: no island was too far from a hungry dragon.

Remaining airborne, Old Fire-Eye circled above the mountains and surveyed his island domain with eyesight keener than an eagle's. Smoke still rose from the last village he had burned several days ago: he had fired every roof before feasting on some half-dozen of their cattle afterwards. Continuing to circle, his gaze became fixed on a single point far below him.

Oho! What was that? Three large ships at harbour. What are they doing here? Time for a closer look.

---oOo---

Nearer now, Old Fire-Eye decided he didn't like what he saw. The ships were about to land more men: soldiers, and lots of them. Time to teach these walking carrion another lesson.

Flapping his wings he soared out to sea before swinging about and beginning to dive: he would burn every ship to the waterline and roast everyone on board. Too many to eat all at once – but he would take the time to scavenge the wrecks for more gems or gold to add to his hoard.

The dragon didn't bother attempting to conceal his approach: and as he neared the ships a cloud of arrows rattled harmlessly off his scales, making him angry. Swinging sharply about, he dragon disgorged a continuous river of flame upon each warship in turn: dragon-fire so hot as to combust all flammables instantaneously. When settling upon the shore in order to contemplate his handiwork, he was surprised by another cloud of arrows: one arrow lodging underneath his left wing. Fire-Eye roared with pain: glaring about him for the culprit.

All the warships remained at anchor, untouched by his flames. The decks were crowded with men – and many archers. Ignoring his pain and half-closing one eye, Old Fire-Eye looked more closely, wondering what had gone wrong.

On the deck of the closest warship, one man stood out prominently. He was dressed in a flowing robe of dark blue, held a staff over his head in both hands, and was chanting in the Old Speech. Ah – a wizard.

Old Fire-Eye responded by exhaling a terrific storm of flame and smoke: the sea-water vaporised when struck and generated huge clouds of steam. But when his flames reached the nearest ship, the wizard's protective magic deflected them harmlessly. Another reason I hate wizards.

Screened from archers by the clouds of smoke and steam, the dragon prepared to launch himself skywards - when he noticed that the previously blue skies had become suddenly overcast. An ominous rumbling filled the air: forked lightning appeared and jumped from cloud to cloud. CRACK! A jagged lightning bolt launched itself and struck the dragon with such force, it felled him to the ground in an agony of rage. Old Fire-Eye thrashed about and screamed – his claws tearing the rocks about him asunder, and leaving deep-gouged furrows: before he rolled himself into the sea.

---oOo---

The dragon re-emerged far out to sea after swimming underwater for quite a distance. Slowly at first, the dragon became airborne and rose rapidly to disappear above the clouds.

The ship's captain approached the wizard anxiously and spoke hurriedly in a low voice. The wizard shook his head, saying nothing: keeping his gaze fixed upon the dragon until it was out of sight. Only then did the wizard turn to answer the captain. "This dragon is a young one: so we can hunt him off the island. The islanders can then remain in peace."

"Aye – hunt the dragon and his gold too!" the captain barked. "Grand it'll be to see my share!" The soldiers nearby laughed in agreement, before dispersing to resume getting ashore to begin their dragon hunt.

Left alone once more, the wizard turned back to stare in the direction the dragon had flown, musing to himself. "Yes - he's young now. But he could well escape us – flying off to to where only dragons can go. With time, he will mature and become strong: then return and seek revenge. For what dragon forgets a single wrong? And when he returns in his strength, what will our sons, and our grandsons, do then?"

The wizard received no answer. All the men about him were too busy: their minds filled with thoughts of dragon-gold.

Dragon-song

Whirl! Whirl in a dragon-flight.

With our beating wings and our clinking scales

Across airy skies, we will drift and sail.

Roar! Roar out into the sky!

For the dragon comes through the evening air

To come as he pleases: let all beware!

Stone! Stone makes our cavern strong.

For our gold and gems are the finest bed

Took from mortal kings while the mortals bled.

Flame! Flame them into a crisp

Greedy thieves who come to rob and steal

Leave their bones to rot, their cold blood congeal.

Mage! Mage – hate the wizard's power.

Though they be but the cleverest sons of men

They cast spells which can harm us and thwart our ken.

Time! Time makes the dragon strong.

Many lives of men makes a dragon great

Grows him strong – to revenge take and glut his hate.

Brarg Lõrth

Brarg Lõrth was a large man. He lived alone, his nearest human neighbours being separated from him by some leagues. His hall was well-built and fenced about by thorny hedges ten feet tall: for Brarg dwelt in the midst of the wilds, and knew how to care of himself.

As a man, he sowed and harvested his wheat and barley, tended his fruit trees, and looked after his bees. His ale was said to be the best this side of the great river. His guests were few: but Brarg liked it that way.

Brarg was grim – but true and leal-hearted. All his animals thought him kind, and they had cause to know.

Brarg hated goblins, hobgoblins, orcs, trolls, and all evil creatures. Goblins abounded under the mountains, but none would cross Brarg's path unless they were numerous and well-armed. But - as goblins preferred the underground, and as Brarg's farm was situated far from the mountains - neither had cause normally to trouble the other.

Brarg was a lot like ordinary men by day: but at night when ordinary men are asleep, Brarg would travel the wilds in a different shape. For Brarg was a shape-shifter, and could take the form a large bear.

As a bear, Brarg met and conversed with other bears. The other bears addressed him rather as bondsmen might address their lord: for Brarg was as wise as he was strong, and the other bruin respected him greatly. While talking to some bears one night, Brarg was told a large band of goblins had just left their mountains on a raid into the woods nearby: bringing their wargs – large black wolves – with them.

Brarg hated the thought of goblins walking about his beloved woods: and like all bears, he hated wargs to the death. As the goblins were numerous, Brarg asked his fellows to go quickly and summon their siblings, parents and cousins - for she-bears fight as savagely as their men. For tonight they would track the intruders down and chase them back to their mountain-holes.

Brarg made his way through the woods like a shadow to sniff out what was happening. Goblin and wargs are easy to track: sure enough, he had only gone a few miles when he picked up their scent, and followed them until he found them milling about in a large glade. The goblins weren't concealing themselves: Brarg heard their yabbering and hollering from a great distance off.

Coming closer, he saw that the goblins had followed and surrounded a few wagon-loads of humans: these had formed their wagons into a circle and built a large bonfire at their centre. From time to time the beleaguered humans flung burning brands into the darkness, setting the fur of incautious wargs alight: who then lit up like torches and fled screaming in pain and scattering all in their path, sowing confusion and mayhem. Brave as the humans were – it was clear they would all be massacred as soon as the goblins organised themselves.

Brarg waited a little, until several score bears had had time to join him down-wind. Before the goblins could rally, Brarg stood up upon his hind legs and roared a challenge so loud it was heard from a league away. His fellow-bears took up his battle-cry, making every goblin within earshot jump out of their skins with terror. With no further need of concealment, Brarg led his comrades forwards through the undergrowth, throwing themselves upon every warg in sight and crushing whatever happened to stand in their way. Whatever wargs survived the onslaught turned tail and fled: whereupon the enraged bears then set about them, striking down goblins with tooth and claw.

The men behind the wagons simply stood there with dangling hands and open mouths – they didn't know yet whether they were being rescued or about to be slaughtered next. Brarg and the others had their hands full, so they didn't stop to explain. The bears hunted down every goblin the met until they came to the foot of the mountain ranges – making further pursuit too dangerous. Then they turned about and vanished back into the woods. The travelers were left alone, in a forest glade that was now eerily quiet; surrounded by the bodies of the slain.

The travelers, as it turned out, were fleeing their serfdom in Mulwraith. They had taken difficult mountain-passes to successfully elude the soldiers looking for them: but the goblins took it to heart that anyone should cross their mountain-lands without permission. The goblins decided to make a point of it – despite the fact that the travelers had by then crossed the mountains and entered the woods - by tracking them down and killing them all.

After Brarg's rescue, the travelers journeyed on until they reached the woodsmen communities up north. There they settled down: but commemorated the night they escaped the goblins each year thereafter with celebrations of dancing, music, ale, and plenty of feasting.

As for Brarg, every animal on his farm noticed that he went about with a huge grin on his face for the next month. But none of them ever did discover what it was that he was so pleased about.

Bear Foot

Bruin sniffing, tasting night-air.

Seeking, seeking, never speaking.

Loping through the forest hunting -

Foes beware!

Bear feet stepping over old ground.

Stalking, stalking, onward walking.

Fording rivers, climbing hillocks,

Moving round.

Bear eyes looking further, out wide.

Sighting, sighting, quickly lighting.

From the hills they look afar

O'er countryside.

Bear claws – daggers danger scorning.

Tearing, tearing, grimly daring.

Rip and crush and break and tear -

Foes take warning.

Wizard Goldir

The old man sat in the highest room of his stone tower, looking out the window and gazing over his tiny island; across to the bay where the sea moved restlessly. He could see the waves murmuring against the stone jetty and his little white boat waiting patiently for him, bobbing up and down against its moorings.

Yes, almost time to leave. So much to do!

The man returned to his reading: old parchments, scrolls, and books covered every spare surface of this room, and even more lined the numerous shelves. Occasionally his silky voice muttered aloud a few words or a short phrase. Once, he raised a hand to describe some characters in the air which continued to shimmer visibly for several moments after the hand was lowered again – finally dissolving into a cascade of sparks.

Goldir was a wizard – and his powers were strong. But the stronger the wizard, the more good – or evil – they can work. Perhaps it was this realisation that caused Goldir to sigh suddenly as he studied, struggling to search out some abstruse subject of mage-craft.

Eventually, Goldir stood and shuttered the windows, before closing and locking the door behind him. Descending the narrow stairs, he arrived at a lower floor which comprised his kitchen, pantry, and larder: a cheerful fire crackled in the fireplace, and the table was soon set. Goldir loved his meat and his ale: and soon indulged his penchant for a large meal.

Later, having finished, he remained seated and began a low sing-song chant while moving one of his hands slowly in a strange pattern. His words ceased, but his hand remained poised mid-air, his eyes closed, brow furrowed. One final movement of his hand caused a living map to spring into existence above the tabletop – whereupon he dropped his hand and opened his eyes

to stare at it intently. The map turned and moved about –
showing miniature people walking, ships sailing, and beasts
herding. Goldir ignored all of the minature activity: his eyes
looking about restlessly for something in particular. Eventually
the map ceased moving and held itself absolutely still. Goldir
hunched forwards, his eyes fixed like those of a hawk upon its
prey.

He knew this island well: the inhabitants named it Gorth,
and he had been there many times. It had one town
encompassed by stone walls and a modest fort, and it was upon
this fort that the wizard gazed for long; not wanting to
acknowledge what his eyes told him. But there was no cause for
doubt: the banners and pennants of the island-lord fluttered
defiantly in the breeze.

The fool will stay after all. Despite all the warnings. Despite
the danger!

Goldir stood up, eyes blazing. The floating map
disappeared. The wizard paced angrily around his kitchen
several times, before forcing himself to stop before the large
window. The sun outside was warm, and the birds were singing.
It was a glorious day.

"I am at fault." he chided himself aloud. "I cannot blame any
man for wanting to defend the home he has always known. He
will – perhaps he should - fight to defend what is his. Even to the
death. Perhaps it is for the best..."

But a cold hand wrung Goldir's heart as he spoke. The
islanders knew – he had told them often - how close the raiders
were. The island lord stood no chance: he knew it as well as the
wizard did himself. Refusing to flee condemned his people to
enslavement: those who were not first slaughtered for resisting in
the first place. Goldir sadly shook his head.

The island-lord of Gorth had just sent him a message:
begging Goldir to come secretly and convey his wife and young
son away to a place of safety. Well, he would go, of course – he
liked the lord of Gorth well enough, despite everything. The
island-lord knew he would die fighting beside his people – but he
still wanted to spare his wife and son. Yes, Goldir would do that
for him.

Why do people make life so complicated?

The wizard left his tower and walked briskly to his boat. He pondered briefly where it was best to take the lady and her son for safe keeping: then shrugged. The lady would make her own decision: for his part, he would convey her to where she wished to go. He would do his part, and save those he could.

Goldir soon sailed out of the little bay: his sail filled with a strong breeze and heading steadily out to sea. For another hour or so its dark blue sail covered with white runes could still be seen from the island: until finally it merged together with the distant sea-haze on the horizon, and disappeared.

Evening came, and the wizrd's tower stood empty. Over the island the birds twittered and sung to themselves, feeding their young: with no thought for the morrow, and taking absolutely no notice of the sordid affairs of mankind.

Mage-Spell

Chanting, speaking, spells of mage -

Read the runes on parchment-page.

Spells of making, spells of fear,

Powers making things appear.

Make arise the crackling flame

Summon shadows with their name!

Speak to beasts and plants and trees,

Walk the wind with gentle ease.

Shape-shift, become beast or bird -

Soar aloft at wizard's word.

Storms a-summon, thunders crack -

Levin-bolts use for attack.

Smoke-wraiths to deceive the eyes,

Mist-shapes weave to fool the wise.

Words command, true naming hear,

Portal open – disappear!

Shadow-Light from Faerie

The isles of Faerie lie far away over the sea to the west. But the faerie-folk do travel abroad: it is said that by magic they can appear almost anywhere, and return again to their island-homes.

Most faerie-folk avoid mankind – but there are exceptions. And so it happened that a Faerie-Lord visited an island he knew to be inhabited only by birds, turtles and seals. On arriving the Faerie-Lord was surprised to discover that a colony of humans had settled there since his last visit. At first he was quite piqued by their audacious lighting of bonfires around their settlement. Wondering what to do about it, he decided to have a closer look, and discovered a tragedy.

The humans that had angered him by settling his island were all gone: and what the Faerie-Lord had taken for bonfires were in fact the burnt-out shells of their buildings. The colony had been raided and its people killed or enslaved. The faerie looked around him with disbelief: how could men so mistreat their fellows? Flying to the shore, he noted a fleet of sails on the horizon – probably the ones responsible for butchering the colony. It was then that he heard a feeble cry.

The Lord soon discovered its source - it came from a babe clutched inside its mother's arms: both lying on the ground at the edge of the village. The mother was dead - a sword-thrust through her body - but the babe was not: though it soon would be, unattended. While the Faerie-Lord knew well enough that most of his kind would have washed their hands of the baby's fate, he adopted a different course: using a sleep-spell to quiet the babe, before summoning a magic cradle to carry the baby all the way back to Faerie-Land.

The Lord engaged a nurse to suckle the babe, who in time grew into a fine boy. He was tutored by a wise elf, and learnt all he might: he was a bright child, and inquisitive. The Faerie-Lord liked the boy well, and the boy in turn regarded the Lord like a well-loved uncle. Near manhood, the boy was told about his own past: which increased his gratitude towards his faerie-uncle, while at the same time hardened his will to revenge himself upon those who had slaughtered his kin.

The Faerie-Lord named the child in his own tongue "Shadow-Light": he foresaw that the child would perform many deeds in dark and dangerous places. Still, his heart was troubled: for he knew that the boy would lose much – perhaps life itself – if he left the isles of Faerie.

When Shadow-Light attained manhood, he asked – as his uncle feared he would – to return to the realm of men. The Faerie-Lord could not deny Shadow-Light the right to pursue his destiny: so with reluctant steps he escorted his adopted nephew to the border of the lands where men dwelt. With a final promise to come to Shadow-Light's aid if summoned, he returned to the faerie-isles with a heavy heart.

---oOo---

Shadow-Light at first concealed his name and travelled. Eventually, he took a ship to the bustling port of Runesai and disembarked to seek for lodgings; for he intended to stay for a time. Runseai was a rough place – being the centre of slave-trading in that region. Once he was cornered by armed thugs: but Shadow-Light had been taught well: with quick movements he suddenly produced two sharp blades – one long, the other short. With them he dispatched two thugs and wounded a third, letting the others flee. After that, Shadow-Light was left alone and did what he pleased.

He didn't remain long in Runesai: he purchased a mid-sized ship and used rather unorthodox methods to recruit his crew. One night he boarded a newly arrived slave-galley, killed its crew and freed the slaves. Most of those freed fled ashore: but some remained with their liberator – taking ship with him and sailing that same night.

Exactly how he managed it all is unknown: but before a year had gone by, somebody calling himself Captain Shadow-Light appeared in the region: intercepting slavers making for Runesai. The Captain killed all slavers he laid hands on, before liberating their cargo and setting them free ashore at the the nearest anti-slaving port.

Captain Shadow-Light's ship fast became the terror of slavers around Runesai: easily recognisable by its dark-blue sails and pennant. It was whispered that Shadow-Light used magic so he could outsail any other ship afloat - even against the wind. The slaves he freed frankly worshipped him as a hero: many served him in some capacity – such as providing with useful information, or crewing on board his ship. Within a few short years his presence overshadowed the region: slave-trade in Runesai dwindled until it threatened to stop completely.

Now the Runesai slavers were still rich: they hired armed escorts and mercenaries to protect their cargoes – but Shadow-Light and his men slew them all, every time. The increased danger made willing mercenaries harder and harder to come by – at any price – so one of the richest slavers thought to provide additional protection by hiring a witch.

The witch was placed aboard a slave-galley attempting to run the gauntlet into Runesai: offering Captain Shadow-Light a bait he could not refuse. Sure enough, some twenty leagues out from Runesai they were pursued by a large vessel with dark-blue sails and fast overtaking them. The slaver's crew and mercenaries paled, while the slaves on board took heart. But the witch waited patiently to spring her trap. And the Captain's ship drew nearer.

When Shadow-Light was close enough, the witch stepped forwards and raised her hands to summon a maelstrom. She used the dark magic to ensure the maelstrom would hunger for human blood: she offered the dark powers which drove the storm Captain Shadow-Light's ship and the lives of his crew. The maelstrom blew up from nowhere in less time than it takes to tell and the Captain's ship began to flounder. Captain- Shadow-Light stood on the prow and attempted to defy the storm: but his magic was not strong enough, and the maelstrom devoured his ship, and all on board.

When the slave-galley arrived at Runesai, the witch was paid, and the slaves marched ashore. But among the slaves went whispers that: as the Captain's boat sank, a winged faerie arrived to pluck a man out of the sea before disappearing. This gave the slaves new hope: and when the slavers heard it, they trembled.

Be that as it may, Captain Shadow-Light was never seen again in the lands of men.

Shadow-Light from Faerie

Shadow Captain

Captain Shadow-Light was a faerie-lad,

And who sailed the wild seas.

And he smashed all chains as he freed the slaves

Trapped in foul slaver's galleys.

He was wild and fey, and a faerie-glow

Oft was seen about his form.

But his freed ex-slaves never cared one wit

For his sake they'd risk all harm.

It was said that he was an ex-slave freed

Who had lost all kin and kith.

He himself said nought. But would draw his sword

And then hew slavers to death.

But a witch-maelstrom came and sunk his boat

And he went down with his crew.

But a few will say, that he was caught up

On his faerie-wings and flew.

But alive or dead, Captain Shadow-Light

Is remembered beyond the grave.

Every slaver fears that he could return

To make free their every slave.

-57-